This book belongs to

Ioha Mackenzie
macDonald

Aged _____

# IN THE

# *Doll's House*

## AND OTHER STORIES

# IN THE
# *Doll's House*
## AND OTHER STORIES

*p*

This is a Parragon Book
First published in 2000

Parragon
Queen Street House
4 Queen Street
Bath BA1 1HE, UK

Copyright © Parragon 2000


ISBN 0-75253-414-9

Designed by Mik Martin

Printed in Spain

These stories have been previously
published by Parragon in the
Bumper Bedtime Series 1999

# CONTENTS

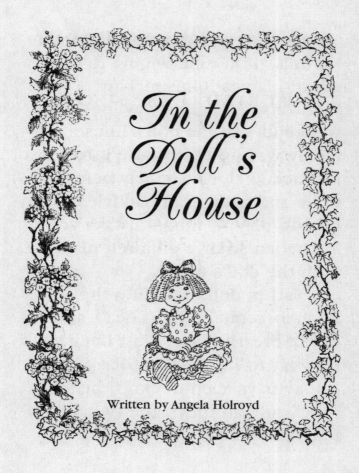

# In the Doll's House

Written by Angela Holroyd

IT WAS SATURDAY MORNING in the doll's house belonging to Clare and James Johnson. The Johnsons had gone away for the weekend, and the doll's house family was upset because it had lost its cuckoo clock. The day before, Clare and James had had friends over to play — things always got lost when strange children played with the doll's house.

Father doll came into the kitchen, scratching his head, and out of breath. "I have just been all the way to Toy Station to ask them if they have seen Cuckoo," he said.

"And had they?" the twins said together.

He shook his head.

"It's too bad," said Mother doll. "I can't do anything without Cuckoo."

"I was going to bake some cakes, but how can I tell when they are done without Cuckoo telling me exactly how long they have been in the oven?"

"I suppose I will have to put all these packets away again," she sighed.

The twins helped her put the flour, the sugar and the currants back into the cupboard.

"I was going to see how fast I could run around the garden," moaned Ben. "But I can't without

Cuckoo telling me how much time I take."

"And Lucy from Toy Farm said I should go over to play at 2 o'clock, but how will I know when 2 o'clock *is* without Cuckoo?" wailed Becky.

"I blame Clare and James," said Mother doll. "They should know by now that the doll's house is always kept neat and tidy, with everything in its place."

"Clare usually checks," said Becky.

"Yes, she remembered to put the dog in his kennel," said Ben.

"Well, she still forgot about Cuckoo," said Mother doll. "And he's far more important."

"I still think he's somewhere in the house," said Father doll. "So I suggest we search every room."

"But why doesn't he answer when we call him then?" asked Becky.

"Perhaps he does," said Father doll. "But we can't hear him."

"He could be lying hurt somewhere," suggested Ben.

"Oh! don't say things like that,"

whimpered Becky. "Quick, we must all go and search. Come on Ben, we'll try the playroom." Ben and Becky raced up to the playroom. It was their favourite room in the whole of the doll's house. There were shelves with plenty of books to read, a table which they did their colouring, cutting and pasting on, and four boxes of toys which they had not played with for some time.

"Perhaps he's been put in one of those and he's stuck," said Ben looking at the bulging toy boxes.

"Let's search through them." They pulled a box each into the middle of the floor and began to work, pulling the toys out one by one.

"Oh! Look!" squealed Becky
with delight. "Here's Mr Clown. I
thought I'd lost him." She pulled out
a brightly coloured, floppy clown.
He had a shiny red nose, a big smile
and wore a spotted bow tie.

"Hey! Look what I've found,"
cried Ben excitedly. He pulled out a
lightly crumpled kite, smoothed it
out and put it next to the clown.

"It's ages since I flew this," he
said.

"That's because the last time you flew it, you let it drop into Toy Farm pond, and then you got it caught up in Mrs Farmer doll's washing and she was very cross," said Becky.

"It wasn't my fault," said Ben. "The wind suddenly dropped."

Ben and Becky continued to search through the two boxes, but Cuckoo was not to be found, so they turned to the next two. Becky found her clockwork train, and Ben found his model aeroplane, but neither found Cuckoo.

"He might have been put in the cupboard," said Becky. This was a cupboard where the bigger toys were kept. They took out the pedal car and the rocking horse and even found their buckets and spades on a shelf at the back, but still there was no sign of Cuckoo.

"Oh dear!" said Becky. "Where can he be?"

"I don't know," said Ben. "But he's not here; we've been through everything."

"So where do we look now?" asked Becky.

Just then Mother doll appeared.

"I've looked through all the other rooms up here," she said.

"We'd better try downstairs then," said Becky.

Becky looked under the cushions

on the sofa. They all looked in the log basket by the fireplace. They looked inside the piano and behind the curtains. They hunted under all of the chairs and under the tables but. . . no Cuckoo!

The cat was the only one not searching — the chair was too comfortable! Mother doll emptied all the sideboard cupboards. She was thrilled to find her favourite, long lost fruit dish hidden behind everything at the back.

"I've looked everywhere for this!" she exclaimed. "We are finding a lot of lost things."

"Yes, but not Cuckoo," said Becky sadly.

They looked under the dining room table and emptied the kitchen shelves. But it was useless.

"I bet those nasty children stole him," wailed Becky.

"Oh, I don't think so," said Mother doll. "Why would they do that?"

"I don't know," cried Becky. By now tears were slipping down her painted cheeks. "All I know is that he's disappeared."

Just then Father doll came in.

"Don't cry Becky," he said. "There is still one place we haven't looked, and I bet those dreadful children played over there too."

"Toy Farm!" they all cried out together.

"Exactly," beamed Father doll.

Ben and Becky walked over to Toy Farm as fast as their stiff little legs would go. Lucy was in the farmyard feeding the chickens.

"Hello Becky," she said "you're early!"

"That's just it," said Ben. "We don't know whether we are late or early, because we can't tell the time anymore."

"Our Cuckoo from the cuckoo clock is missing!" blurted out Becky. "Those terrible children who came to play with Clare and James yesterday obviously put him somewhere."

"Oh! Those two horrors. We've had lots of trouble today trying to find all our animals because of them," said Lucy.

"The cows were in the stables. The horses were in the cowshed. The sheep were in the pigsty and the pigs were in Ma's vegetable patch."

Ben, Becky and Lucy looked all over the farm, even in the tractor shed, but Cuckoo was nowhere to be seen. Suddenly Ben had a brilliant idea.

"If those children didn't know the difference between cows and horses, I bet they didn't know the difference between a cuckoo and a duck," he shrieked, racing off to the duck pond.

"Why didn't we think of that before!" chorused Becky and Lucy. And sure enough there on the edge of the pond was Cuckoo.

"Cuckoo!" screamed Becky and Ben together. "We've searched everywhere for you. Why didn't you come home?"

"Because I've been enjoying myself talking to my new friends," said Cuckoo. "You've no idea how bored I get stuck in that clock day in and day out — no one seems to even notice me."

"Oh! Cuckoo. You silly bird," cried Becky. "We haven't been able to do anything without you."

"It's true," said Ben. "We all need you very much and if you come home with us now, we promise to let you come back and see the ducks from time to time."

Cuckoo was delighted. He had found new friends and realized that he was important all on the same day. The doll's house dolls were also delighted — now their lives could get back to normal.

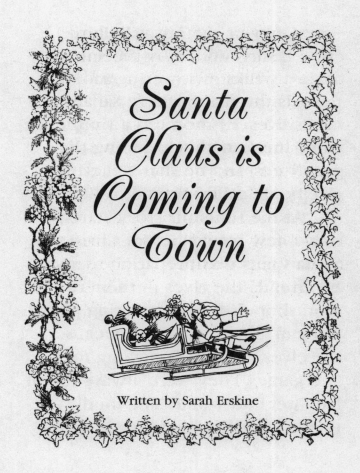

# Santa Claus is Coming to Town

Written by Sarah Erskine

DEEP IN a faraway valley, surrounded by the snowy peaks of towering mountains, is the place where Santa Claus lives. His home is a simple log cabin, nestled snugly among the pine trees, and he shares it with a sleepy cat called Fireside.

At the time our story starts, only a few weeks before Christmas, Santa Claus was preparing to visit his friends the elves in their workshop. It was an exciting place to be at Christmas time, because the elves were busy making toys and games. They were always full of laughter and would sing loudly as they dashed back and forth with

pieces of wood and pots of paint.
Santa Claus liked to go and watch
them working and perhaps join in
with the singing if he could
remember the words.

With a tug that nearly made
him topple over, Santa put on his
boots. He struggled into his heavy
coat, and wrapped a thick scarf
around his neck. Then he pulled his

favourite red, woolly hat down over his ears, because it was always his ears that got cold first.

Santa stepped out into the white, crunchy snow, took a deep breath of fresh, mountain air, and began the walk to the workshop. He followed a narrow, winding path between the pine trees and saw the rays of sunlight make the snow glisten. He trod carefully over a small bridge and looked down to see the icy blue water as it tinkled over smooth pebbles. As he walked, he hummed a happy tune and thought about Christmas Eve, for it was the most exciting time of the year for Santa Claus. It was the night of *The Great Delivery of Presents* to all the children who had been good and well-behaved.

In the distance, Santa could see the workshop but he could not hear the elves singing or laughing.

"Perhaps the wind is carrying the sound away," he thought, and he carried on happily humming. But as he drew closer, he *could* hear the elves — instead of laughter, he heard angry shouting!

Santa quickened his pace and threw open the door of the workshop. Inside, a sorry scene met his eyes. Two of the elves, Bright and Chuckles, were standing in the middle of the room, both clutching the same comic book and refusing to give it up.

"Let go of my book!" shouted Chuckles.

"It's not yours!" yelled Bright. "It's mine!"

"Bright! Chuckles!" cried Santa. "Whatever is the matter? Why are you arguing like this?"

"Chuckles took my book," howled Bright.

"I did not!" bellowed Chuckles, angrily.

"But can't you share your things like you usually do?" Santa asked them.

"No!!!" shrieked both the elves at once, and they pulled the book so hard that it ripped right down the middle.

"Now see what has happened," sighed Santa. "Because you were both being selfish, you have spoiled the book for everyone.

"I don't care," pouted Chuckles.

"It was a stupid book anyway," said Bright.

Santa looked unhappily at the workshop. It was usually clean and tidy, but toys and books had been thrown everywhere and he could even see an old sandwich that had been squashed into the carpet. Some of the elves still lounged half-asleep in their beds, while others sat throwing things at each other and being rude. Santa could also see that they had not made any toys or gifts for *The Great Delivery of Presents.*

"Why are you behaving like this?" asked Santa. "The children are going to be so disappointed if there are no presents for them."

The biggest elf, whose name was Sprite, looked up at Santa with a frown.

"We don't care about the children," he said. "None of the

children does as he or she is told,
so we don't see why *we* should."

"Oh, dear me!" sighed Santa,
and he shook his head sadly. "I
know that there are some bad
children in the world, but most of
them are good. So if *you* are being
too naughty to make any toys, then
I shall jolly well make them myself!
Now I had better go and see how
the reindeer are getting on. They
will be very sad to hear how
naughty you are being."

Santa turned and slowly left the
workshop. Behind him he could
hear the raised voices of the elves
as they began quarrelling and
squabbling again.

The wind was cold. It tugged at Santa's clothes as he trudged through the snow to the stables where the reindeer lived. Snow flakes settled on his beard, and instead of looking at the beautiful scenery around him, he stared gloomily at his boots.

Inside the stables it was warm and cozy. Lanterns hung from the ceiling and gave out a golden glow. But Santa looked about and was dismayed to see that all the harnesses, which hung upon the walls, were dirty and unpolished. The silver bells that were used to decorate the sleigh were tarnished and dull instead of bright and shiny.

Even the sleigh itself sat in a dark and dusty corner, covered in cobwebs and bits of straw. It was obvious that the reindeer had done nothing in preparation for *The Great Delivery of Presents*. In fact, they were all sitting or standing in front of the fire doing nothing at all.

"Why aren't you getting ready for Christmas?" Santa asked them anxiously.

One of the reindeer looked sadly at Santa.

"There isn't going to be a delivery this year, Santa," he moaned.

"Don't be silly," laughed Santa.

"I shall make some toys myself and we can still do the delivery.

"Haven't you read the news?" the reindeer grunted, and nodded his head toward a newspaper. Santa picked it up and read the front page. In big black letters the headline read

Santa gasped. The report said that children everywhere were being rude, grumpy, disobedient, selfish, and unkind. Santa could hardly believe it. He slumped into a chair and put his head in his hands.

He could only deliver presents to children who were good. If there were no good children, Santa would be out of a job, and he didn't know how to do anything else. He had once tried to be a plumber, but he caused so many floods that he had to give it up.

Santa sat and thought, shaking his head sadly every now and then. Suddenly he jumped up.

"I'm not going to believe what

it says in the newspapers!" he cried. "I think that there must be some good, kind children in the world."

"You're wasting your time, Santa," sighed another reindeer. "I bet you won't be able to find a single good child anywhere."

"Well, I think I can," said Santa. "It's my job, after all." And he left the stables and crunched back through the snow to his cabin.

Going straight to one of the shelves, he took down a huge roll of paper called *The Great Map of Everywhere*. It was too big to fit on the table, so he spread it out over the floor. Then he held a pin high above his head, and made big circles in the air with it.

Closing his eyes tight, Santa stuck the pin into the map. He opened his eyes to see where it had landed because, wherever it was, that would be the place where he would begin his search for the one good child. He looked down at *The Great Map of Everywhere* and ...

"Oh dear me!" chortled Santa. "The pin has landed in the sea. There won't be any children there. I'll have to try again."

So again Santa closed his eyes, waved the pin in the air and stuck it into the map. This time it had landed in a place called Greenville.

"Then Greenville is where I shall go!" announced Santa loudly, making Fireside jump in surprise. Wasting no time, Santa wrapped an extra scarf around his neck, pulled his hat down over his ears again, and said goodbye to Fireside.

Outside the cabin, Santa tipped back his head and looked at the sky. It was late in the afternoon and beginning to get dark.

"Excuse me!" he called up to a cloud. "Are you going anywhere near Greenville!"

"Why yes," the cloud called back. "I'm on my way there now to deliver some snow. I can take you there, if you like." And the cloud lowered itself down to the ground, sprinkling a flurry of white snow-flakes as it came. Santa climbed aboard and the cloud sailed up and away. They were soon high over the trees and mountains. The stars winked in the dark night sky and, looking down, Santa could see the tiny, twinkling dots of light from the towns and cities below. Santa snuggled deep into the fluffy cloud and soon fell fast asleep. He dreamed of hot chocolate pudding and of trees that grew toffees.

When Santa awoke it was morning, and the cloud had already sprinkled a thick layer of snow over Greenville Town. Stretching and yawning, Santa thanked the cloud for a lovely journey and waved goodbye as it sailed back into the sky. Then he stood and looked around

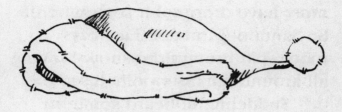

Greenville was a small town with some shops, a park and playground, and streets of snug, snow-covered houses. Santa took a notebook and a short, stubby pencil out of his pocket, and set off to find some nice children so that he could make a list of their names. As he walked, his ears began to feel very cold, and putting his hand up to his head he realized that his hat had gone.

"Oh dear me!" he tutted. "I

must have dropped it somewhere." So Santa began to retrace his footsteps through the snow looking all around for his woolly hat.

Suddenly he heard someone crying. He looked up and saw a girl leaning out of her bedroom window. Her face was angry and red with rage.

"Whatever is the matter?" Santa called up to her. The girl looked down and when she saw Santa she scowled. She did not recognize him without his red, woolly hat.

"I'm not allowed out to play!" she wailed.

"Why not?" asked Santa.

"Because I made a mess of my

bedroom and threw my toys everywhere!" she sobbed.

"Oh well," laughed Santa. "I'm
sure you'll be able to play if you
tidy your room quickly."

"But I don't want to!" she
shouted rudely, and she slammed
the window shut!

"Goodness me!" said Santa. "I
don't think that little girl can go on
my list." And he carried on walking
down the street.

As he was passing a garden he
saw a boy kicking a garbage can
furiously. When Santa asked him
what the matter was he carried on
kicking and spoke in a loud,
grumpy voice.

"I've got to look after my little-sister because my mum's not well and it means I can't play football with the other boys."

"But surely you don't mind if your mother's not well?" Santa was very surprised.

"Little sisters aren't any fun and it's not fair!" the boy complained.

Santa walked on and on, but he could not find his red, woolly hat or any nice children. They were, as the newspaper had said, rude and bad-tempered. His ears were getting colder and colder, so he went into a shop to buy a new hat, but they had completely sold out of red, woolly ones. As Santa left the shop he noticed a big sign outside the Santa's Toyshop. It read,

CLOSED
NO
SANTA
THIS YEAR

Santa walked around the playground and then around the park and after a while he sat down on a bench. His ears were very cold, and he rubbed them with his hands to try and warm them. He looked at his notebook, but there were still no names in it. Feeling very cold, hungry, and miserable, Santa decided that the reindeer must have been right. There was not a single good child left.

"I shall have to go home," he thought unhappily, "and start looking for another job." And he rubbed his ears again in an effort to warm them up.

"Excuse me," said a small voice by his side, "but are your ears cold?"

"Yes, they are," said Santa, looking round to see a small boy standing beside him. "Have you seen a red, woolly hat anywhere?"

"No," replied the little boy. "But you can have mine." And promptly he took off his hat and handed it to Santa. Santa tried putting it on, but it was too small.

"My Dad has a hat that he never wears," said the little boy. "Why don't you come to my house for tea and we'll ask if you can borrow it. We're going to have hot chocolate pudding and custard, and mum said that I could bring a friend home if I wanted."

"Chocolate pudding! Why that would be lovely!" cried Santa and his eyes twinkled happily. At last he had found a child who was good and kind-hearted. "I must put you on my list," he said excitedly, introducing himself. The boy said that

his name was Evan, and that he was
very pleased to meet the real
Santa Claus. Then they shook hands
and began walking through the
snow.

When they arrived at Evan's
home, Santa shook hands with
Evan's father and gave a deep bow
to his mother, and they told Santa
that any friend of Evan's was a
friend of theirs. They all sat around
the fire and Santa's ears got warmer
and warmer as he ate the hot

chocolate pudding. Soon Santa had told them all about the elves and the reindeer, and how difficult it was to find any nice children.

"Why don't you take Evan to the workshop to prove that not all children are horrible?" suggested Evan's father. Evan smiled a huge smile.

"Would you like that?" asked Santa.

"I'd love to!" said Evan, and he became so excited that he could hardly sit still. Evan's mother agreed that he could go, and while she made them a flask of hot coffee for the journey, Santa went outside to call another cloud. He looked up, and there was the same snowcloud that had given him a ride the night before.

"I've been looking for you," called the cloud. "You left your hat behind." And sure enough, when Evan and Santa climbed on to the cloud, there was the red, woolly hat. Santa quickly pulled it right down over his ears and the two of them laughed about it for the whole journey.

When Santa and Evan arrived in the faraway valley, they went straight to the elves' workshop. It was even more untidy now and the elves were still fighting and arguing with each other. Evan looked at them all and then he said in a very loud voice:

"Is it fun being so naughty?"

Suddenly, the workshop went very quiet. The elves stopped what they were doing and looked at Evan in stunned silence.

"Of course it's fun!" snapped Bright, angrily. "We don't have to do what we're told, we can make a mess, we can even stay up all night if we want to. We can all do exactly what we want." Bright scowled at the other elves to make sure that they agreed. Then, in the quiet, there suddenly came the sound of sobbing. It was coming from the top of one of the bunk beds.

"I... I... I don't think it's fun," said a small, wobbly voice, and the pink, tear-stained face of Tot, the smallest elf, appeared from underneath the bedclothes. "We don't play nice games anymore, because nobody plays fair," he gulped. "And I miss making toys for all the children. And the reindeer aren't friends with us. And Santa doesn't like us any more. And I don't want to stay up all night because I get too tired. And nobody laughs ... and ... and nobody hugs me any more." With that, poor little Tot burst into tears again and burrowed his face into his pillow. And then, one by one, all the other elves burst into tears as well.

"We're sorry, Tot," wailed Chuckles. "We didn't mean to make you unhappy. And you're right, being bad isn't that much fun after all."

All the elves gave Tot a hug. And then they hugged Santa, and then Evan, and then they hugged each other and Chuckles even tried hugging himself, but he fell over and started laughing. Soon, all the other elves were laughing too and

they began straight away to tidy the workshop.

"We want to make lots of lovely presents for Christmas now," said Chuckles, "but who will you give them to, Santa? Evan is the only nice child you managed to find."

"Don't you worry. There must be lots of other good children," laughed Santa. "I shall find them." So Chuckles ran to tell the reindeer that Christmas was going ahead as usual and everyone began working furiously to get ready for *The Great Delivery of Presents.*

Evan caught a fast cloud back to Greenville and told all his friends

about Tot and the other elves. The children felt guilty about having been so badly behaved and they also realized that it was more fun to be good because people liked them more. Gradually the news spread and children everywhere started being good and kind and feeling a lot better for it.

Santa flew over the towns and cities, and soon he had enough names to fill a hundred notebooks.

Meanwhile, the reindeer cleaned and scrubbed and brushed. The sleigh was given a new coat of paint and they polished the harnesses until they shone. The silver bells sparkled like diamonds and tinkled a merry tune.

In the workshop, the elves were busy sawing, hammering, painting, and wrapping. In one

corner there was a pile of presents
that grew bigger and bigger with
each passing hour. Every one of
them worked as hard as they could,
and by Christmas Eve everything
was ready. The elves gathered
outside to wave and cheer the
sleigh goodbye as Santa left to start
*The Great Delivery*.

The reindeer pranced and

danced through the sky, pulling Santa and all the presents behind them. And at the very back of the sleigh was an extra special present for a little boy called Evan who had made them all realize that being good and kind was much more fun than being horrid!

The Magic Tree

TOMMY RUBBED his eyes, blinked hard, and looked out of his bedroom window again. But it was still there — an enormous oak tree that definitely hadn't been there yesterday! If it had been there, he'd have known all about it for sure. For a start he would have climbed up it, for Tommy loved nothing better than climbing trees.

No, this tree was definitely not there yesterday! Tommy sat staring at the tree in wonder and disbelief. The tree stood there, outside his bedroom window, with its huge, spreading branches almost asking to be climbed. Tommy wondered how on earth it had suddenly got there, but he decided that before he wondered about that too much, he had better go and climb it first. After all, there was always time later to wonder about things but never enough time to do things, he thought.

As soon as he was dressed, he ran outside to take a closer look at the new tree. It seemed just like any other big oak tree. It had lots of wide, inviting branches and lots of green, rounded leaves. And it had deep, furrowed bark just like any other oak tree.

Tommy couldn't resist any longer. On to the lowest branch he stepped and then up to the next. The tree seemed so easy to climb. There were branches everywhere. In no time at all, he was in a green, leafy canopy. He couldn't even see the ground any more. But something seemed not quite right. The branches beneath his feet seemed to be so big

now that he could stand up on them
and walk in any direction. And the
branches all around him seemed just
like trees themselves. In fact, he
suddenly realised that he wasn't any
longer climbing a tree, but standing
in a whole forest full of trees.

Tommy didn't like this at all, and
thought he had better get down. But
where was down? All he could see
were tall, swaying trees and here and
there a twisty path leading off even
deeper into the forest. Tommy didn't
know how he had done it, but he
had somehow got himself
completely lost in a forest, and he
hadn't even had breakfast yet!

Worse still, it seemed to be

getting dark. "Quick, over here!" a voice suddenly called out. Tommy was very startled, but he was even more startled when he saw that the voice belonged to a squirrel.

"You can speak!" blurted out Tommy.

"Of course I can speak!" snapped the squirrel. "Now listen. You are in great danger, and there's no time to lose if we are to save you from the clutches of the evil Wizard of the Woods."

The squirrel quickly explained that, long ago, a spell had been cast on the forest and it had become enchanted. Every now and again, the Wizard of the Woods, who ruled the forest, lured an unsuspecting person into his realm by making a tree appear. Once you climbed the tree, you entered the forest. Escape was almost impossible.

"But why does the Wizard of the Woods want to lure people into the forest?" asked Tommy, rather hoping that he didn't have to hear the answer.

"To turn them into fertilizer to make the trees grow," said the squirrel.

Tommy didn't really know what fertilizer was, but it sounded rather nasty. He was pleased when the squirrel suddenly said, "There is just one way to get you out of here. But we must hurry. Soon it will be dark and the Wizard of the Woods will awake. Once he awakes, he will smell your blood and he will capture you."

With that, the squirrel jumped up the nearest tree. "Follow me," he said.

Tommy immediately climbed after the squirrel. "Where are we going?" he panted as they climbed higher and higher.

"To the top of the tallest tree in the forest," the squirrel answered as they clambered from tree to tree, climbing ever higher.

"But why?" asked Tommy.

"Because that's the only way to escape. You'll see!" said the squirrel.

Eventually they stopped climbing. They were at the top of the tallest tree in the forest. Below them and around them was nothing but more trees. Tommy looked up, and at last he could see the clear, twilight sky. He also noticed something rather strange. All the leaves at the top of the tallest tree were enormous.

"Quick, time is running out," said the squirrel. "Sit on this leaf and hold tight."

Tommy sat on one of the huge leaves. The squirrel whistled, and

before Tommy could blink he had
been joined by a hundred more
squirrels. They each took hold of the
branch to which the leaf was
attached. With a great heave, they
pulled and pulled until the branch
was bent backwards. Suddenly they
let go. With a mighty "TWANG", the
branch, with Tommy and the leaf
attached, sprang forward. As it did so
Tommy and the leaf were launched
into the air. High above the trees
they soared until, ever so slowly, they
began to float down to earth. Down,
down, they went, until they landed
with a bump.

Tommy opened his eyes to find
himself on his bedroom floor. He ran

over to the window and looked out. The magic tree was nowhere to be seen. It had gone as quickly as it had appeared. But perhaps it had never been there at all. Maybe it was just a dream. What do you think?

# A Woodland Home

WHEN THISTLEDOWN the elf decided to move out of his parents' home in the trunk of a tree, he knew just what he was looking for. He had always liked the idea of living in a toadstool house. Some elves these days think that those red and white dwellings are gaudy and not in the best possible taste, but Thistledown thought he would feel like a grown-up elf if he lived in one. The only problem was finding the right property.

Elves do not really have estate agents, but they do have home-finders, who usually know what kinds of houses are available in the local area. Young Thistledown trotted along to see the nearest friendly homefinder straight away.

"What kind of property are you looking for?" asked the plump homefinder, making notes on an official-looking clipboard.

Thistledown explained how much he liked toadstool houses.

"Then I have just the right thing for you!" exclaimed the homefinder. "Come along with me right now, for it will be in great demand."

The homefinder, whose name was Locket, led Thistledown deep into the wood, where some of the trees were old and rotten, while others had fallen and lay across the paths.

"It's not a very fashionable neighbourhood," said the young elf, looking about him.

"It is very competitively priced to take account of that," said Locket severely, "and the price you are prepared to pay is … well … shall we say *modest*?"

Thistledown felt that he had been put firmly in his place, but he was a sensible young elf and kept an open mind about the house he was going to see.

At last, Locket stood still and gestured dramatically.

"Here you are!" he said. "As you

can see, it is part of a terrace of three homes."

Thistledown looked carefully at the very fine toadstools standing at the base of an old tree. He rubbed his eyes and looked again.

"But there are no doors or windows!" he cried.

Locket consulted his clipboard. "As it says here," he said, "these

toadstools are absolutely *ripe* for conversion."

But Thistledown shook his head vigorously.

"No," he said. "I am definitely looking for something that I can move into right away. And I really do think that I should like to live in a better part of the wood. I wouldn't want my visitors to be worried about being attacked by owls when they came to see me. Besides, it's very dark here. I'd like to see the sunshine from time to time. That is essential."

Locket hugged his clipboard to his chest.

"I can see that you are going to

be a very demanding client," he said, "but it's my job to find you what you are looking for. There is another house I'd like you to see. It's not exactly a toadstool, but I think you will find it full of traditional charm."

Thistledown wasn't at all sure what this meant, but it turned out to be the way that Locket described a damp, dark, tree-root house very near to the rejected unconverted toadstools.

"No," said Thistledown. "This isn't what I am looking for at all."

Over the next few days, Locket took Thistledown to see over thirty possible places. All of them, in Thistledown's view, were absolutely dreadful. There was a tree-trunk house that was so ramshackle a great chunk of bark came off in his hand. There was a toadstool house that a family of black beetles had already occupied. Thistledown had a particular horror of black beetles, ever since one of them had crawled into his acorn bed when he was a baby. There was also a disused bird's

nest, which had fallen to the ground, a tiny cave that looked as if it would get flooded whenever it rained, and a little cottage with no roof.

"That is the last property I have to show you," said Locket. "I wonder if you are being quite realistic about your requirements, young man. When it comes to choosing a home, you do sometimes have to compromise."

Thistledown said that he quite understood about compromise, but he really couldn't live in anything he had so far seen.

"I'll know it when I see it," he said of his dream home. "And then I won't hesitate, believe me."

Thistledown's parents were

secretly very happy that their son had not yet found a suitable house. They did not really want him to move out.

"When you have saved up some more, it will be easier," said his father. "It's always hard setting up home for the first time. I remember it well."

"You weren't by yourself," retorted Thistledown's mother. "You were already married to me, and we would never have found our first home if it had been left up to you!" She winked at Thistledown. "You follow your dream, son," she said. "There are plenty of people who will try to persuade you to settle for second best. Don't you listen to them, will you?"

So Thistledown continued to look at possible homes, and he continued to be disappointed. As the weeks passed, he became more and more depressed.

"Perhaps it would be better if you found a home of your own, if this is how you're going to be," said his father unsympathetically, when Thistledown had mooched into the house in a miserable way for the fourth time that week.

"That's exactly the trouble," muttered Thistledown.

The next day, however, he really did try to pull himself together. He decided to take himself off for a long walk, to clear his head and raise his plunging spirits.

In fact, it was a beautiful day. The sun sparkled through the leaves, and little woodland animals were scampering and chattering wherever he looked. It was the kind of day on which it felt good to be an elf, and young Thistledown began to feel better. What was he complaining about? He already had a safe, warm home, where he was welcome to stay as long as he needed. One day, he would find the home of his own that he was dreaming about, and until that day came, things were really not so bad.

Thistledown breathed in the warm, woodland air. He kicked his heels in the clearings and twizzled around the trees. Then, quite suddenly, he saw something that made his heart stand still. It was a perfect toadstool house.

Thistledown stood with his mouth open for a moment. The little house was exactly what he had imagined. It had two little windows and a tiny door. Its roof was red and white, just as toadstool roofs should be.

As Thistledown stood there, staring at the little house, the door opened, and a very pretty elfin girl came out to shake crumbs from a

tablecloth. She saw Thistledown at once and smiled at him.

"Can I help you?" she asked. "Were you looking for someone?"

"Yes, no, yes!" said the young elf.

"Well, which is it?" laughed the girl, folding her tablecloth.

"I was looking for a something, not a someone," said the elf.

"What sort of a something?" The girl looked puzzled.

"A house!" cried Thistledown. "Your house is the most beautiful I have ever seen."

"Well, thank you," said the girl, looking a little pink. "I am very fond of it myself. It was given to me by my favourite aunt, who had to move away. I'm very lucky to own such a lovely home." Then Thistledown found himself telling the girl all about his own quest. She was amazingly easy to talk to, and before long, she had invited Thistledown in to have some dandelion tea.

Over the next few days, the young elf's parents noticed that his step became lighter and his smile came more easily. It was not long before he introduced them to the reason for his happiness and told them that he and his new friend had decided they would like to get married.

So although Thistledown is now living in his dream home, he does not think it's the most important thing in the world. In looking for a something, he *did* find a someone, and that is better than anything.

# Toot! Toot!

OLD LADY LOOSESTRIFE of Goblin Hall was a very light sleeper. She often tossed and turned until the early hours of the morning, before she finally drifted off to dreamland. Perhaps it was because she did not get as much sleep as she needed that Lady Loosestrife was always in a terrible temper.

Servants at Goblin Hall changed as often as the sheets. Very few of them could stand the way that Lady Loosestrife shouted at them all day long. She was never satisfied with the way that work was done.

Even when the tables had been polished so that you could see every detail of your face in them, the mistress of Goblin Hall was full of fury.

"I told you to use lavender scented beeswax!" she would yell. "This is lily of the valley, and it smells horrible. Do it again, every inch!"

But no one suffered as much as Lady Loosestrife's chauffeur Buggles. Strangely enough, he had been in her employment longer than any of the other servants at the hall. His father had been chauffeur before him. And before that, his grandfather had driven Lady Loosestrife's father in a very grand carriage.

Lady Loosestrife had never taken driving lessons, and she had not the

first idea about the rules of the road or the workings of a motor vehicle. But that didn't stop her. She regularly told Buggles to change into sixth gear (when he only had five) and instructed him to drive across red traffic lights. But Buggles was perfectly calm. He did what he thought was right and totally ignored Lady Loosestrife, which was just as well, for she could single-handedly have caused more traffic accidents than the rest of the inhabitants of the country put together.

More than anything else, Lady Loosestrife wanted Buggles to hoot his horn at other traffic and at passers-by. In her heart, she felt that she alone should be allowed to use the road, and other drivers and pedestrians should keep out of her way. If she had only known, other drivers and pedestrians did keep out of her way. They didn't want to be shouted at, and although Buggles was a very good and steady driver, who knew when he might be pushed too far and actually follow his mistress's instructions? It was not a risk worth taking.

Nevertheless, some people, of course, did have to use the roads at the same time as her ladyship. They had their livings to earn after all. Then Lady Loosestrife would scream at poor Buggles.

"Hoot at that man! He's wearing horrible trousers. It shouldn't be allowed! Hoot at that driver! How dare he have a purple car like mine? Hoot at that dog! I just know it would bite me if it could. Hoot at that policeman! His uniform buttons aren't fastened properly!"

You see, Lady Loosestrife believed that everybody's business

was her business, and her business was nobody else's business at all.

Now Buggles very rarely hooted and tooted at other road users. He knew it was just as likely to cause accidents as any of Lady Loosestrife's other driving instructions. He just calmly went along at his own pace

and ignored her ladyship. But that
seemed to make her even crosser.
One day she saw something in a
catalogue that she felt would
improve her chauffeur's driving
enormously. It was a claxon — a
kind of hooter-tooter that made an
incredibly loud noise.

Next time she went out in her
car, Lady Loosestrife popped the
claxon into her huge handbag.

As usual, Buggles wasn't doing
nearly enough hooting and tooting
as far as his passenger was
concerned.

"Hoot at that woman in the
preposterous hat!" screamed Lady
Loosestrife. "It's too ridiculous and

much too much like one of mine. Hoot at that man with the bicycle! He looks as if he's about to wobble. Hoot at that woman with the twins! She had no business having two children at once. The very idea! Hoot at that cow. Hoot! Hoot!"

But Buggles just drove on. Driven to distraction by his failure to hoot and toot, Lady Loosestrife pulled the claxon out of her bag and opened the window. Oh dear! What an awful commotion! The preposterous hat blew off in the blast, hitting the man on the bicycle, who not only wobbled but fell off, right in the path of the woman with the twins, who immediately began to scream, upsetting the cow and causing her to run straight down the road and through the open window of the fishmonger's shop.

Lady Loosestrife, oblivious to the mayhem she was causing, sailed on in her car, hooting her claxon at every opportunity. In this way, she blazed a trail of destruction through the countryside, and the disasters that occurred in her wake came to the notice of the local constabulary.

"That woman must be stopped," said the Chief Inspector. "I want road blocks at every junction. Poor old Buggles, it isn't his fault, but something has got to be done about Lady L."

The operation that was mounted to stop the claxon-blowing menace was bigger than any ever seen in the county. It didn't take long before Buggles, much to his mistress's disgust, pulled up at a signal from a policeman standing in the middle of the road.

"Don't stop! Don't stop!" yelled her ladyship. "He shouldn't be in the middle of the road. It serves him right if he's run over." And she blew her claxon several times just to show that she meant business.

But Buggles drew to a stop and wound down the window to talk to the officer.

"It's all right, Buggles old son,"

said the policeman. "It's not you we want. I'm afraid we're going to have to arrest Lady Loosebox there, for use of an offensive claxon and causing a breach of the peace."

I will leave you to imagine Lady Loosestrife's fury at:

1. Being taken into custody;
2. Being called Lady Loosebox;
3. Having her claxon confiscated;
4. Finding that Chief Inspectors don't follow orders from members of the public, and
5. Having to wait in a cell with a burglar, a poacher and the poacher's dog.

Lady Loosestrife told the Chief Inspector that she had every

intention of buying another claxon
as soon as she got home. The Chief
Inspector said that as far as he was
concerned, she could buy as many
claxons as she liked, but she was on
no account to use one. He also
mentioned the fact that next time
she might have to share a cell with a
murderer and that no special

arrangements were made in prison for members of the aristocracy.

"What, no servants?" asked Lady Loosestrife, shocked to her very marrow.

"Absolutely no servants," said the Chief Inspector, "and no caviar, champagne or Buggles."

Lady Loosestrife was silent for longer than she had been in many a long year. She agreed to be bound over to keep the peace and went rather quietly back to her car.

"Just a minute, Buggles," said the sergeant at the desk. "I've wanted to ask you something for ages. Just between you and me, how do you stand it?"

Buggles didn't pretend not to know what he meant.

"Oh, that's easy," he said. "After the first year of screaming, my hearing was so bad, I had to have a hearing aid. It has a very efficient volume control

IF HE HAD said it once, he had said it a hundred times. Poor Farmer Forrest was in despair. At any time of the day you might see him look up from his work towards the top meadow and cry in exasperation, "Now where's that sheep?"

Yes, Molly was a sheep who loved to wander. She wasn't a stay-at-home-and-wait-for-your-wool-to-grow kind of sheep at all. At the sight of a lowish wall, a thinnish hedge or a weakish fence, Molly was off. She didn't run or make a noise or draw attention to herself in any way. She simply trotted off down the lane. It was sometimes hours before anyone noticed she was gone at all.

But after her fourth escape attempt, Farmer Forrest became wise to Molly's ways. He put her in the top meadow, where he could keep an eye on her. Whenever he lifted his eyes from his work, he checked to see that she was there. But still the

cry was heard at least once a week. "Now where's that sheep?"

To be fair, it wasn't really Molly's fault. You see, Farmer Forrest didn't keep sheep as a rule. He had cows, pigs and a few hens, but he had never farmed sheep. It was only when Mrs Forrest took up spinning that she begged her husband to invest in a flock.

"But I don't know anything about sheep!" complained her husband. "Besides, this isn't the right kind of country for them. No one for miles around has sheep. Can't you just buy a fleece to spin?"

But Mrs Forrest argued that it just wouldn't be the same. To spin wool from a sheep that had lived on your own land, that would be really satisfying.

"And I can just see you wearing the jumper I would knit," she told her husband. Think how proud you would be."

"All right," said Farmer Forrest, "but not a whole flock. We'll start with one sheep and see how we get on. That's only sensible."

Mrs Forrest reluctantly agreed, but in fact this was very far from sensible. You see, sheep are sociable animals. They like to be with a whole group of their own kind. They're not loners at heart. That was why Molly set off to find some like-minded sheep at every opportunity. As I said, it really wasn't her fault.

But Farmer Forrest found that he was wasting an enormous amount of time running around the countryside looking for that sheep. She nearly always trotted off in the same direction, as she had a strong feeling that there were other sheep to the north of her, but even so, there were many winding lanes around Forrest Farm, and it sometimes took the farmer the best part of a morning to find her.

"You know," Farmer Forrest said to his wife, "this can't go on. You'll have to find somewhere else to supply you with wool. I can't keep spending time running after that sheep. I'm far too busy at this time of year."

"Oh, but if you could just wait another couple of weeks, pleaded Mrs Forrest, "it would be time to shear her. Once I've got my fleece, you can sell her if you like, although I must confess that I've become rather fond of Molly. She's got such an independent spirit."

"Independent spirit my big toe!" scoffed her husband. As soon as she's shorn, that sheep can go and be independent somewhere else."

A couple of days before the shearing, as Mr and Mrs Forrest

were sitting at breakfast, Mrs Forrest raised the subject again.

"Honeybun," she began.

"Don't call me that," growled Mr Forrest.

"How would you like a whole flock of sheep like Molly?"

"We've been through this before," said Mr Forrest. "I've told you, I am not a sheep farmer."

"Well," said his wife, pointing with her cereal spoon, "I think you are now."

Mr Forrest followed her gaze. Up in the top meadow was a flock of sheep. Not one lonely Molly but at least fifteen sheep.

"What on earth...?" Mr Forrest

hurried from his chair and threw on his coat. This had to be sorted out.

But when he drew near the meadow, he found that his eyes had not been playing tricks on him. There really were fifteen sheep grazing happily on the juicy grass. And only one of them was Molly. To be honest, despite his many trips across the countryside to bring her

home, Mr Forrest wouldn't have been quite sure which sheep *was* Molly, but Mrs Forrest had followed him from the farmhouse, and she at once pointed out their own sheep.

"But where have these others come from?" asked Mr Forrest. "None of them have markings or collars or tags as far as I can see."

"I haven't the faintest idea," said his wife. "We'll have to think how we can find out who owns them. They do look *lovely* up here though, don't they?"

Mr Forrest grunted and went off to his work, while Mrs Forrest hurried back to the farmhouse.

The telephone was ringing as she arrived.

"Oh, Deidre," said a voice. "Thank goodness I've caught you. Something dreadful has happened. We've lost Hortense."

Mrs Forrest recognised the voice of one of the members of her spinning circle.

"Hortense?" she queried. "Is that your daughter?"

"No, no, no," cried the caller. "It's my sheep. The one I was going to have sheared next week. How am I going to find her?"

"Well, you could ask my husband," suggested Mrs Forrest. "He's had quite a lot of experience of finding sheep, especially just lately."

But even as she was speaking, Mrs Forrest was getting the funny feeling that she had seen Hortense rather more recently than her friend had.

"Let me call you back," said Mrs Forrest. "I just need to check something out."

Over the next few minutes, Mrs Forrest telephoned six of her spinning-circle friends. Every one of them reported a sheep that had gone missing during the past night. The farmer's wife felt pretty sure that other members would report a similar event.

"Oh, *clever* Molly," breathed Mrs Forrest. She realised now that the sheep must have made several friends in a similar situation as she roamed the countryside on her many bids for escape.

The sheep were so happy all together in the meadow that no one had the heart to send them all home — even Farmer Forrest. So Mrs Forrest became the official shepherdess of the spinning circle.

I wouldn't like to promise that Molly has wandered off for the last time, though. I did hear that there was a solitary sheep over in Farmbridge. And if I heard it, I expect Molly did too…

ONCE UPON A TIME, there was a group of boys who played in a band. They practised very hard and soon became so good that they were always invited to perform at the village fête in the summer and for the carol-singers in the winter. And very often, during the year, they would be asked to play a few tunes at a party, or a wedding, or a ceremony at the village hall.

Everyone was happy. The boys made lots of pocket money (which was just as well, because instruments are very expensive), and the village had its own little band it could call on.

There was only one problem,

and that was Eddy. Now Eddy played the trumpet like an angel. *That* wasn't the problem. He could sing beautifully too, and sometimes did a chorus of *Silent Night* when the band trotted round the village with the carol-singers. In almost every way, Eddy was a perfect member of the band, if only he wasn't always late!

It didn't matter how carefully the boys discussed their arrangements beforehand, when they called at Eddy's house on the edge of the village, it was always the same.

"Are you ready, Eddy?" they would shout.

"Nearly," Eddy would call back,

and the other boys would groan, because they knew what "nearly" meant. It didn't mean, "I've just got to put my socks on and I'll be with you." It didn't mean, "I'm running down the stairs right now." It didn't even mean, "Just let me comb my hair and clean my shoes and I'll be there." It meant, "Sometime in the next hour or so, I might be ready to join you."

As you can imagine, it drove the other boys absolutely wild. They had tried everything to solve the problem. Bobby had been appointed Eddy's "minder", responsible for making sure he was ready, but after two weeks, Bobby resigned. He couldn't bear the mess in Eddy's bedroom, and he couldn't bear the vague way in which Eddy did everything at home. When they were playing, it was quite different. Eddy always came in at the right places and had his wits about him. At home, he was a different boy.

"I know just how you feel, Bobby," said Eddy's mother, when she found Bobby sitting in despair at the bottom of the stairs, waiting for her son.

"I don't know what to do about him. He just doesn't seem to have any idea of time," she went on. "Getting him to school in the morning is a nightmare. We'll make

superhuman efforts to have his
clothes and shoes ready. I'll stand
over him until he's brushed his teeth
and combed his hair. Then I'll just

leave him to put his tie and shoes on. You wouldn't believe that a boy could take an hour to do something as simple as that."

"I would," groaned Bobby. "Oh, I would."

This state of affairs went on for so long that everyone had become used to it. The boys in the band took to calling for Eddy at least two hours before he was needed. By hanging around outside and shouting up to his window every ten minutes, "Are you ready, Eddy?" they would eventually manage to get him out of the house.

Eddy's mother grew used to getting up a couple of hours early to get her son off to school. It was ridiculous, but no one could see another way to do it.

Then Eddy's Uncle Albert came to stay. He wasn't a real uncle, in fact. He had gone to school with Eddy's father and had long been a friend of the family. Eddy had called him Uncle Albert since he was tiny.

Now Uncle Albert had not visited for several years, as he had been working abroad, so he did not know about Eddy's lateness. He was shocked the first morning of his visit to find his hostess downstairs at the crack of dawn. Eddy's mother explained the whole problem.

The next day was a Saturday, so

Uncle Albert looked forward to being able to sleep in without being disturbed, but once again he was woken horribly early. He came muttering out of his room to find Bobby waiting patiently on the stairs. There was a wedding at nine o'clock, and Bobby was making quite sure that Eddy wouldn't be late, as he was playing a solo.

Uncle Albert sat down on the stairs with Bobby and listened to the whole story.

"But this is ridiculous!" he said. "Haven't you tried to stop it? You can't let it go on."

So Bobby told Uncle Albert about all the efforts that had been made to improve Eddy's timekeeping. He explained that Eddy had been talked to, pleaded with, shouted at, encouraged and even rewarded, but that nothing had worked.

"I see," said Uncle Albert. "Have you tried doing nothing?"

"Well," said Bobby, "that's what we're doing now, really."

"No, no," said Uncle Albert. "I mean nothing as in *not* arriving early for him."

"But he'll be late," said Bobby.

"Yes," said Uncle Albert. "But at least then he'll realise the consequences of his actions. He's not a bad lad, but I don't think at the moment he has any idea how much trouble people go to for him."

"You're probably right," said Bobby. "But we can't start today. The wedding…"

"Yes, yes, I understand," said Uncle Albert. "But we will start on Monday. Agreed?"

Bobby told the band about the new plan, and Uncle Albert told Eddy's mother.

The boys in the band agreed that it was worth a try.

"After all," said Bobby, "nothing else has worked."

Eddy's mother looked doubtful, but she was at her wits' end.

"Frankly, Albert," she said.

"I'm willing to try anything. I'll leave it in your hands."

On Monday morning, no one shouted at Eddy to get ready for school. So he was late. By the time he finally wandered into the schoolyard, it was already time for morning break. His teacher told him not to let it happen again and gave him extra work.

On Monday evening, Eddy was so late for band practice that the other boys had gone home before he arrived. Eddy felt a little annoyed at this. They could have waited just a few minutes, couldn't they?

On Tuesday morning, Eddy was late for school again. This time the teacher was not so understanding. He gave Eddy extra homework and a lecture about punctuality.

On Tuesday evening, the band was supposed to be playing "Happy Birthday" to Mrs Marlow, who had celebrated her hundredth birthday that day. Luckily it was a tune that sounded all right without the trumpet, because Eddy failed to turn up at all.

On Wednesday morning, Eddy made an effort to get to school on time. It wasn't a very successful effort, because he was still twenty minutes late for his first class, but it was a start.

That evening, Eddy arrived at

band practice about five minutes before it ended. Things were slowly improving.

It took three weeks, and a really quite unpleasant session with the headmaster, before Eddy began to arrive at school on time. With no one to shout at him, being punctual for band practice took a little longer, but it happened in the end.

Now, it has become a tradition that the band stands in front of their trumpeter's house and calls, "Are you ready, Eddy?" But there is never any reply, for Eddy is down in the street shouting too!

# Buried Treasure

JIM LIVED in a big old house with a big rambling garden. The house was rather spooky, and Jim much preferred the garden. He would spend hours kicking a football around the overgrown lawn, climbing the old apple trees in the orchard or just staring into the pond in case he might spot a fish.

It was a wonderful garden to play in but Jim was not really a happy child because he was lonely. How he wished he had someone to play with! It would be such fun to play football with a friend, or have someone to go fishing with. He had plenty of friends at school, but it was a long bus journey to his home and besides, his school friends found his house so spooky that they only came to visit once.

One day Jim was hunting about in the garden with a stick. He hoped he might find some interesting small creatures to examine. Every time he found a new creature he would draw

it and try to find out its name. So far, he had discovered eight types of snails and six different ladybirds. As he was poking about under some leaves he saw a piece of metal sticking out of the ground. He reached down and pulled it free. In his hand lay a rusty old key. It was quite big, and as Jim brushed away the soil, he saw that it was carved with beautiful patterns.

Jim carried the key indoors and cleaned it and polished it. Then he set about trying to find the lock that it fitted. First he tried the old garden gate that had been locked as long as Jim could remember. But the key was far too small. Next he tried the grandfather clock in the hall. But the key did not fit the clock's lock. Then he remembered an old wind-up teddy bear that played the drum. Jim hadn't played with the toy for a long time and he eagerly tried out the key, but this time it was too big.

Then Jim had another idea. "Perhaps the key fits something in the attic," he thought. He was usually too scared to go into the attic on his own because it really was scary. But now he was so determined to find the key's home that he ran up the stairs boldly and opened the door. The attic was dimly lit, dusty and full of cobwebs. The water pipes hissed and creaked and Jim shivered.

He began to look under a few
dustsheets and opened some old
boxes, but didn't find anything that
looked like it needed a key to unlock
it. Then he caught sight of a large
book sticking out from one of the
shelves. It was one of those sorts of
books fitted with a lock. Jim lifted
down the book, which was
extremely heavy, and put it on the
floor. His fingers trembled as he put

the key in the lock. It fitted perfectly.
He turned the key and the lock
sprang open, releasing a cloud of
dust. Jim wiped the dust from his
eyes, slowly opened the book and
turned the pages.

What a disappointment! The
pages were crammed with tiny
writing and there were no pictures
at all. Jim was about to shut the book
again when he heard a voice. The
voice was coming from the book!
"You have unlocked my secrets," it
said. "Step into my pages if you are
looking for adventure."

Jim was so curious that he
found himself stepping on to the
book. As soon as he put his foot on

the pages he found himself falling
through the book. The next thing he
knew he was on the deck of a ship.
He looked up and saw a tattered
black flag flying from a flagpole and
on the flag were a skull and cross-
bones. He was on a pirate ship! He
looked down and saw that he was
dressed like a pirate.

The pirate ship was sailing along
nicely, when suddenly Jim saw some

dangerous-looking rocks in the water — and they were heading straight for them! Before he could shout, the ship had run aground and all the pirates were jumping overboard and swimming to the shore. Jim swam, too.

The water felt deliciously warm and when he reached the shore he found warm sand between his toes. He couldn't believe it! Here he was on a desert island. The pirates went in all directions, searching for something to make a shelter. Jim looked, too, and under a rock he found a book. The book looked familiar to Jim. He was sure he'd seen it somewhere before. He was still puzzling over it when one of the pirates came running towards him waving a knife. "You thief, you stole me rubies!" cursed the pirate in a menacing voice. What was Jim to do?

Then he heard a voice call out from the book, "Quick! Step into my pages." Without thinking twice, Jim stepped into the book and suddenly he was back in the attic again.

Jim peered closely at the page from which he'd just stepped. The Pirates and the Stolen Treasure it said at the top of the page. Jim read the page and found he was reading exactly the adventure he had been in. He turned excitedly to the contents page at the front of the

book and read the chapter titles.
Journey to Mars, he read, and The
Castle Under the Sea. Further down
it said: The Magic Car and Into the
Jungle. Jim was thrilled. He realised
that he could open the book at any
page and become part of the
adventure, and he only had to find
the book and step into it to get back
to the attic again.

After that, Jim had many, many adventures. He made lots of friends in the stories and he had lots of narrow escapes. But he always found the book again just in time. Jim was never lonely again.

LONG AGO there lived a poor farmer called Fred, who had a horse called Rusty. Once Rusty had been a good, strong horse. He had willingly pulled the plough and taken his master into town to sell his vegetables. Now he was too old to work on the farm, but the farmer couldn't bear to think of getting rid of him because he was so sweet-natured. "It would be like turning away one of my own family," Fred used to say. Rusty spent his days grazing in the corner of the field. He was quite content, but he felt sad that he was no longer able to help the poor farmer earn his living.

One day, Fred decided to go to

town to sell a few vegetables. He harnessed Beauty, the young mare, to the wagon and off they went. Beauty shook her fine mane and tossed a glance at Rusty as if to say, "Look who's queen of the farmyard!"

While Fred was in the town, his eye was caught by a notice pinned to a tree. It said:

# HORSE PARADE
## at 2 pm today

### *The winner will pull the King's carriage to the Grand Banquet tonight*

"There's not a moment to lose, my girl!" said Fred. "We must get you ready for the parade." So saying, he turned the wagon around. "Giddy-up, Beauty!" he called, and she trotted all the way back to the farm.

Fred set to work to make Beauty look more lovely than she had ever done before. He scrubbed her hoofs and brushed her coat until it shone. Then he plaited her mane and tied it with a bright red ribbon. Rusty watched from the field. "How fine she looks," he thought, wistfully. "She's sure to win." He felt a bit sad that he was too old to take part in the parade, so he found a patch of the sweetest grass to graze on, to console himself.

All at once, he heard Fred approach. "Come on, old boy," he said, "you can come, too. It'll be fun for you to watch the parade, won't it?" Rusty was thrilled. It seemed such a long time since the master had last taken him into town.

Fred brushed Rusty's coat, too. "You want to look your best, don't you now, old boy?" he said.

Soon the three of them set off back into town, with Fred riding on Beauty's back and Rusty walking by their side. When they reached the parade ground, there were already a lot of horses gathered there with their owners. There were horses of every shape and size — small, skinny ones, big, muscular ones and there were even big, skinny ones, too!

Soon it was time for the parade to begin. The king entered the parade ground, followed by the members of the royal court. They took their places at one end of the ground. Then the king announced three contests. First there would be a race. The horses would gallop from one end of the parade ground to the other. Then there would be a contest of strength. Each horse would have to try and pull a heavy carriage. Lastly, there would be a trotting competition. Each horse would have to carry a rider around the parade ground.

The competition began. All the horses lined up at the starting line. "Come on, Rusty. Have a go!" whispered Fred. He led Rusty and Beauty to where the other horses were lined up.

All the other horses turned and

stared. "What's an old horse like you doing taking part in a contest like this?" one of them asked disdainfully.

"You won't make it past the starting line!" taunted another.

Rusty said nothing and took his place at the start. Then they were off down the field. Rusty felt his heart pounding and his feet fly like never before, but try as he might he just couldn't keep up with the others and came in last.

"What did you expect?" snorted the other horses turning their backs on poor old Rusty.

However, Rusty was not downcast "Speed isn't everything," he said to himself.

Now it was time for the test of strength. One by one the horses took it in turns to pull the carriage. When it was Rusty's turn, he tried his best. He felt every muscle in his aching body strain, as he slowly pulled the carriage along.

"Not a hope!" declared the other horses.

"Strength isn't everything," said Rusty to himself.

Next it was time for the trotting competition. "I shall ride each horse in turn," declared the king. He climbed up on to the first horse, but it bolted away so fast that the king was left hanging by the stirrups. The next horse lifted his legs so high that he threw the king right up in the air and he might have hurt himself badly, if he hadn't been caught by one of his courtiers. The next horse was so nervous about carrying the king that his teeth chattered, and the king had to put his fingers in his ears. Then it was Beauty's turn and she carried the king magnificently, until she stumbled at the end. At last it was Rusty's turn. The other horses sniggered, "Let's see that old horse make a fool of himself!"

Rusty carried the king quite slowly and steadily, making sure he picked his feet up carefully, so that his royal highness would not be jolted.

"Thank you for a most pleasant ride," said the king dismounting. There was a hush as the horses and their owners awaited the result of the contest.

"I have decided," announced the king, "that Rusty is the winner. Not only did he give me a most comfortable ride, but he accepted his other defeats with dignity. Speed and strength are not everything, you know."

Rusty and Fred were overjoyed, and even Beauty offered her congratulations. "Though I might have won if I hadn't stumbled," she muttered.

So Rusty proudly pulled the king's carriage that evening, and he made such a good job of it that the king asked him if he would do it again the following year. Then the king asked Fred if his daughter could ride Beauty from time to time. He even gave Fred a bag of gold to pay for the horses' upkeep. So the three of them were happy as they never had been before as they returned home to the farm that night.

# The Boy Who Wished Too Much

THERE ONCE WAS a young boy named Billy. He was a lucky lad, for he had parents who loved him, plenty of friends and a room full of toys. Behind his house was a rubbish tip. Billy had been forbidden to go there by his mother, but he used to stare at it out of the window. It looked such an exciting place to explore.

One day, Billy was staring at the rubbish tip, when he saw something gold-coloured gleaming in the sunlight. There, on the top of the tip, sat a brass lamp. Now Billy knew the tale of Aladdin, and he wondered if this lamp could possibly be magic, too. When his mother wasn't looking

he slipped out of the back door,
scrambled up the tip and snatched
the lamp from the top.

Billy ran to the garden shed. It
was quite dark inside, but Billy could
see the brass of the lamp glowing
softly in his hands. When his eyes
had grown accustomed to the dark,
he saw that the lamp was quite dirty.
As he started to rub at the brass,
there was a puff of smoke and the

shed was filled with light. Billy closed his eyes tightly and when he opened them again, he found to his astonishment that there was a man standing there, dressed in a costume richly embroidered with gold and jewels. "I am the genie of the lamp," he said. "Are you by any chance Aladdin?"

"N… n… no, I'm Billy," stammered Billy, staring in disbelief.

"How very confusing," said the genie frowning. "I was told that the boy with the lamp was named Aladdin. Oh well, never mind! Now I'm here, I may as well grant you your wishes. You can have three, by the way."

At first Billy was so astonished he couldn't speak. Then he began to think hard. What would be the very best thing to wish for? He had an idea. "My first wish," he said, "is that I can have as many wishes as I want."

The genie looked rather taken aback, but then he smiled and said, "A wish is a wish. So be it!"

Billy could hardly believe his ears. Was he really going to get all his wishes granted? He decided to start with a really big wish, just in case the genie changed his mind later. "I wish I could have a purse that never runs out of money," he said.

Hey presto! There in his hand was a purse with five coins in it.

Without remembering to thank the genie, Billy ran out of the shed and down the road to the sweet shop. He bought a large bag of sweets and took one of the coins out of his purse to pay for it. Then he peeped cautiously inside the purse, and

sure enough there were still five coins.

The magic had worked! Billy ran back to the garden shed to get his next wish, but the genie had vanished. "That's not fair!" cried Billy, stamping his foot. Then he remembered the lamp. He seized it and rubbed at it furiously. Sure enough, the genie reappeared.

"Don't forget to share those sweets with your friends," he said. "What is your wish, Billy?"

This time Billy, who was very fond of sweet things, said, "I wish I had a house made of chocolate!"

No sooner had he uttered the words than he found that he was

standing outside a house made
entirely of rich, creamy chocolate.
Billy broke off the door knocker and
nibbled at it. Yes, it really was made
of the most delicious chocolate that
he had ever tasted! Billy gorged
himself until he began to feel quite
sick. He lay down on the grass and
closed his eyes. When he opened
them again, the chocolate house had
vanished and he was outside the
garden shed once more. "It's not fair
to take my chocolate house away. I
want it back!" he complained,
stamping his foot once again.

Billy went back into the shed.
"This time I'll ask for something that
lasts longer," he thought. He rubbed

the lamp and there stood the genie again.

"You've got chocolate all around your mouth," said the genie disapprovingly. "What is your wish?"

"I wish I had a magic carpet to take me to faraway lands," said Billy. No sooner were the words out of his mouth than he could feel himself being lifted up and out of the shed on a lovely soft carpet. The carpet took Billy up, up and away over hills, mountains and seas to the end of the Earth. He saw camels in the desert, polar bears at the North Pole and whales far out at sea. At last, Billy began to feel homesick and he asked the magic carpet to take him home.

Soon he was back in his own garden again.

Billy was beginning to feel very powerful and important. He began to wish for more and more things. He wished that he did not have to go to school — and so he didn't! He wished that he had a servant to clear up after him and a cook to make him special meals of sweet things — and a cook and a servant appeared.

Billy began to get very fat and lazy. His parents despaired at how spoiled he had become. His friends no longer came to play because he had grown so boastful.

One morning, Billy woke up, looked in the mirror and burst into tears. "I'm so lonely and unhappy!" he wailed. He realised that there was only one thing to do. He ran down to the garden shed, picked up the lamp and rubbed it.

"You don't look very happy," said the genie, giving him a concerned glance. "What is your wish?"

"I wish everything was back to normal," Billy blurted out, "and I wish I could have no more wishes!"

"A wise choice!" said the genie. "So be it. Goodbye, Billy!" And with that the genie vanished. Billy stepped out of the shed, and from then on everything was normal again. His parents cared for him, he went to school and his friends came to play once more. But Billy had learned his lesson. He never boasted again and he always shared his sweets and toys.

# The Chocolate Soldier

IN THE WINDOW of Mrs Brown's sweet shop there stood a chocolate soldier. He had chocolate ears, chocolate eyebrows and a curly chocolate moustache of which he was particularly proud. But best of all he loved his shiny foil uniform with its braid on the shoulders and cuffs, and smart red stripes down each leg. All day long the chocolate soldier stood to attention on a shelf in the window, staring straight ahead out into the street.

Standing next to him on the shelf were more chocolate soldiers, and beyond them he could see some sugar mice and a twist of liquorice bootlaces.

It was summer time and the sun shone through the window of the sweet shop. At first the chocolate soldier felt pleasantly warm; then he started to feel uncomfortably hot. Next he began to feel most peculiar indeed. His chocolate moustache was wilting and his arms were dripping. Soon he was completely melted and before he knew it, he had slipped out through a hole in his silver foil shoe and was pouring off the shelf and out into the street.

Down the street he poured.

"Stop! Help!" he shouted, but nobody heard his cries. Now he could hear the sound of gushing water and, to his horror, he could see he was heading for a stream at the bottom of the street.

"Help me! I can't swim! I'm going to drown!" the chocolate soldier cried as he plunged into the cold, running water. But now something very strange was happening. He found he could swim quite easily. He looked round and saw that he had a chocolate tail covered in scales. He looked down at his arms, but there was a pair of fins instead. The cold water had hardened him into the shape of a chocolate fish!

The chocolate soldier was carried downstream, and after a while the stream broadened out and became a river. He realised that he would soon be carried out to sea.

"Whatever shall I do?" wondered the chocolate soldier. "I'm sure to get eaten by a bigger fish or maybe even a shark!" He tried to turn around and swim against the river's flow but it was no good. The current swept him away down river again.

Soon he could see the waves on the shore. He smelt the sea air and tasted the salt in the water. Now he found himself bobbing up and down on the sea. He could see a boat not far away and then all of a sudden he felt a net closing around him. He struggled to get out, but the net only tightened and soon he felt himself being hauled out of the water and landed with a "thwack!" on the deck among a pile of fish. The smell was awful, and the chocolate soldier was quite relieved when he felt the boat being rowed towards the shore.

"I'll hop over the side as soon as we land and run away," he thought, quite forgetting that he had no legs but only a fish's tail.

But there was no chance of escape. As soon as the boat reached the shore, he and all the other fish were flung into buckets and lifted into a van. The van stopped outside a shop and a man carried the buckets inside, where it smelt of fried fish, chips and vinegar. The chocolate soldier found himself being lifted up with a lot of other fish in a huge metal basket. He looked down and saw a terrible sight below. They were heading for a vat of boiling oil! At that very moment he felt very peculiar once again. His scales melted, his tail drooped and he felt himself slide through the holes in the basket and into the pocket of a man's overalls.

The chocolate soldier lay in the corner of the pocket, while the man worked all day in the shop. Then the man headed for home, with the chocolate soldier bouncing up and down in the overall pocket as the man walked along. Soon they arrived at the man's house. He reached into his pocket.

"Look what I've found," he said to his small son. "A coin. Here, you can have it — but don't spend it all at once!" he said, chuckling to himself. The chocolate soldier felt himself being passed from one hand to another.

"So now I've hardened into the

shape of a chocolate coin," he thought. "And I'm going to be eaten by the boy!" But to his surprise he found himself being slipped into the boy's pocket.

The chocolate soldier felt himself bouncing up and down in the child's pocket as he ran up the street and into a shop. The chocolate soldier peeped out and to his astonishment saw that he was back in Mrs Brown's sweet shop. Then he realised what was happening. The boy believed he was a real coin and was going to try and spend him! The boy stood in the queue at the counter.

The chocolate soldier called out

to his soldier friends in the window, "Pssst! It's me! Help me get out of here!" One of the soldiers looked down, but all he could see was a chocolate coin sticking out of the boy's pocket. Then he recognised the voice.

"I'm a chocolate soldier like you, but I've been turned into a coin. Help!" cried the chocolate soldier.

"Leave it to me," replied the soldier on the shelf. "Don't worry, we'll have you out of there in a jiffy!"

The word was passed along and, quick as a flash, one of the sugar mice chewed off a length of liquorice bootlace. Then the soldier lowered the lace into the boy's pocket, where it stuck to the chocolate coin. Carefully the soldiers hauled the coin up on to the shelf. The chocolate soldier was delighted to find his foil uniform was still there on the shelf, just where it had been before. All the effort of getting on to the shelf had made him quite warm, and he found he could slip quite easily back through the hole in the shoe and into his uniform again.

"I'd like a chocolate soldier," said the boy to Mrs Brown. But when he reached in his pocket the coin had gone.

"Never mind," said kind Mrs Brown, "I'll let you have one anyway."

She reached into the window and took down a soldier from the end of the row and gave it to the boy. And as for our chocolate soldier? In the cool of the night he turned back into a smart-looking soldier again.

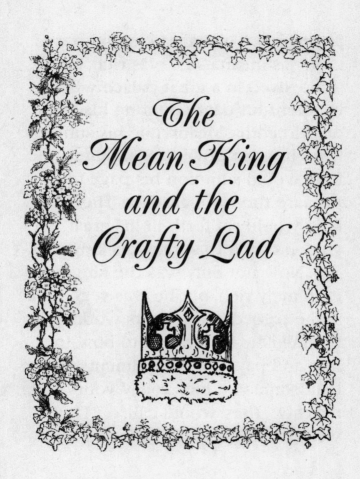

# The Mean King and the Crafty Lad

THERE WAS ONCE a king who was as mean as he was rich. He lived in a great palace where he spent his days counting his bags of gold coins. Meanwhile his subjects lived in great poverty. Sometimes the king would summon his page to prepare the royal carriage. Then the king would set forth in his great, golden coach to survey his kingdom.

Now not only was the king extremely rich, but he was very vain. As he passed his subjects working in the field, he liked them to bow to him and pay him compliments. "How handsome you look today, your majesty!" they would call, or "How well the colour pink suits you, Sire!"

His head would swell with pride as he moved on. "My people truly adore me!" he would say.

But for all their complimentary words, the people hated their king. They resented the fact that the king lived in splendour while his subjects toiled hard all their lives. At last a secret meeting was called among the peasants.

"Let's sign a petition demanding our rights!" cried one man.

"And fair pay!" shouted another. They all cheered and clapped their hands.

"Who's going to write down our demands?" called an old woman. Now the crowd was hushed, for none of them knew how to read or write.

"I know what we can do instead," called a voice from the back. Everyone turned round to see a young lad in rags. "Let's march on the palace!" he cried.

"Yes!" roared the crowd.

As the angry mob reached the palace, the king saw them and sent out his guard dogs. The peasants were forced to flee for their lives with the dogs snapping at their ankles. Not until the last peasant was out of sight did the king call off his dogs. "Good work!" he cried.

From then on, however, life became even harder for the people because the king was on his guard in case they marched on the castle again. Now, when he went out and about in his kingdom, he was always accompanied by his hounds.

Eventually, another secret meeting was called. "What can we do?" the people said. "We will never be able to get past those savage dogs."

"I've got an idea," came a familiar voice. It was the ragged lad again. For a while there was uproar as folk accused him of having nearly lost them their lives. "Please trust me," pleaded the lad. "I know I let you down, but this time I've got a well thought-out plan to get the king to give up his money." In the end, the peasants listened to the boy's scheme and decided to let him try.

The next day, the boy hid in a branch of a tree that overhung the palace garden. With him he had some dog biscuits, in which he had hidden a powerful sleeping pill. He threw the biscuits on o the palace lawn and waited.

Some time later, as the boy had hoped, the king's hounds came out on to the lawn. They headed straight for the biscuits and gobbled them up. Soon they were fast asleep, one and all.

Quickly the lad slid out of the tree and, donning a large black cape, he ran round to the front of the palace and rapped on the door. A sentry opened the door. "Good day," said the lad, "I am Victor, the world-famous vet. Do you have any animals requiring medical attention?"

"No," replied the sentry, slamming the door in the lad's face. Just then voices could be heard from within the palace.

After a few moments, the sentry opened the door again and said, "As a matter of fact, we do have a bit of a problem. Step inside."

The sentry led the lad out to the lawn where the king was weeping over the dogs' bodies.

"Oh, please help," he cried. "I need my dogs. Without them I may be besieged by my own people."

The lad pretended to examine the dogs. He said to the king, "I have only seen one case like this before. The only cure is to feed the animals liquid gold."

"Liquid gold?" exclaimed the king. "Wherever shall I find liquid gold?"

"Fear not," said the lad, "I have a friend — a witch — who lives in the mountains. She can turn gold coins into liquid gold. You must let me take the dogs — and a bag of gold — to her and she will cure them."

Well, the king was so beside himself with fear that he readily agreed. The sleeping dogs were loaded on to a horse-drawn cart, and the king gave the lad a bag of gold saying, "Hurry back, my dogs are most precious."

Off went the lad, back to his home. His mother and father helped him unload the dogs, who by now were beginning to wake up. They took great care of the dogs, who

were glad to be looked after kindly for once. The next day the lad put on the cloak again and returned to the palace.

"The good news is," he said to the king, "that the cure is working. The bad news is that there was only enough gold to revive one dog. I'll need all the gold you've got to cure the others."

"Take it all," screamed the king, "only I must have my dogs back tomorrow!" He opened the safe and threw his entire stock of gold on to another cart, which the young lad dragged away.

That night the lad gave each of the king's subjects a bag of gold. The next morning he led the dogs back to the palace. To his surprise, the king didn't want them back.

"Now I have no gold," he said, "I don't need guard dogs."

Then the lad saw that the king had learned his lesson, and he told the king what had really happened.

And to everyone's joy, the king said the peasants could keep their bags of gold. As for the king, he kept the dogs as pets and became a much nicer person.